SESAME STREET
123

W9-AYD-421

Zoe's Day with Daddy

By Sarah Albee and P.J. Shaw
Illustration by Tom Brannon

Dalmatian Press, LLC, 2008. All rights reserved.
Published by Dalmatian Press, LLC, 2008. The DALMATIAN PRESS name and logo are trademarks of Dalmatian Press, LLC, Franklin, Tennessee 37067. No part of this book may be reproduced or copied in any form without written permission from the copyright owner.

Printed in the U.S.A.
ISBN: 1-40374-327-4

08 09 10 11 BM 10 9 8 7 6 5 4 3 2 1
17121 Sesame Street 8x8 Storybook: Zoe's Day with Daddy

It was almost time for Zoe to go to school. She was humming and tapping a spoon against her cereal bowl.

"Zoe, how would you like to go with Daddy to the office today?" said her mother. "It's Take Your Little Monster to Work Day."

"Don't joke me!" Zoe exclaimed.

"It's true," said her father. "You can go to work with me today."

So Zoe said, "Okay!"

"Look at the clothes I picked, Mommy," Zoe said. "I'm not going to wear my tutu today. I'll wear my office outfit instead."

Zoe pulled on a pink top with tiny hearts.

"This will be cool!" she said. "We can draw with markers, and Daddy can show me his computer!"

Zoe's mother gave her a kiss. "Good-bye, sweetie. Have a good day with Daddy."

"Whoa, wait a minute. Hold the phone," Zoe said suddenly. "I can't miss school today! We're going to learn about shapes."

"Don't worry," said her father. "Your teacher said it was okay. My office has lots of different shapes. We'll learn about them together."

"When we get there, can I make a paperclip necklace and swivel around in your chair?" Zoe asked her father. "As long as you're quiet as a mouse," he replied.

"I can be a mouse, Daddy. Hey, I bet you don't know the
answer to this," she snickered. "What's a mouse's favorite game?"

When they got to the office, Daddy made a
special place for Zoe to sit, right beside his desk.

"That box is made of rectangle shapes," he told her.
"Each rectangle has four sides and four corners."
"I like rectangles," said Zoe, "but I like circles better.
When is circle time?"

"Grown-ups don't have circle time," her father explained. "But here's a pencil and some paper so you can draw pictures of circles." He held up the paper. "What shape is this paper, Zoe?"

"I know," she said. "A rectangle! It has four corners and four sides. Two sides are long, and two are short."

"That's right," Daddy said. "You know, a square is kind of like a rectangle. Both have four sides, but a square has sides that are all the same length."

"Is it almost time to go outside and play?" Zoe asked after a while.

"Uh, no, honey," said her father. "Grown-ups don't have recess. Would you like to fill this cup with water so you can water my plant?"

Zoe nodded and took the cup.

"You can tell your teacher the cone-shaped cup was kind of like a triangle," Daddy said. "Triangles have three sides and three corners."

"Telly says triangles are fas-cin-a-ting," Zoe giggled.

"When is snack time?" Zoe asked, after watering the plant.
Her father was talking on the telephone, so he opened a
drawer and handed Zoe a roll of mints.
"Have one of these," he whispered.

The mints were circle-shaped, but they didn't taste as good as the round cracker snacks at school.

Finally, Zoe's father hung up the phone. "Lunchtime!" he said cheerfully.

"Yippee!" cried Zoe. "Show me to the pizza!"

They headed to the cafeteria.

"Well, honey, they're not serving pizza today," said Daddy, helping Zoe with her tray. "Sometimes they serve things in grown-up cafeterias that kids aren't used to eating. But just because it's new doesn't mean it's not delicious."

"Really?" said Zoe. She decided to try the tomatoes and broccoli. Broccoli looked like a little tree!

After lunch, Zoe plopped down again at her desk.

"We take a nap at school," she yawned. "But I'm a big girl today. No nap, right?"

"I could use a nap myself," her father smiled. "But you're right. At a grown-up job, you don't take naps. Here, why don't you rest and make a paperclip necklace while I go to my meeting?"

Zoe loved necklaces!

So Zoe made a necklace for her mommy and a red rubberband ball for Elmo.

"The paperclips are like little ovals, and the ball is round," she thought. "I'll tell Elmo his ball is shaped like a circle."

Finally, it was time to go home.

"So, how did you like going to work with me today?" asked Zoe's father.

Zoe did a little pirouette. "I don't like the office as much as school, but it was fun being with you. And I found lots of shapes, too!"

"I have an idea," Daddy suggested. "Let's put some pieces of paper, the cup, a paperclip, and the rubberband ball in your box, and we'll take them to school tomorrow to show off what we learned together."

"Thank you, Daddy. We'll be in great shape!" Zoe joked.

When Zoe gave Elmo his ball the next day, Elmo said, "Wow! That's the best rubberband ball Elmo ever saw! Did Zoe like going to the office?"

"It was neat," she said. "I really liked Take Your Little Monster to Work Day. But, Elmo, you know what's *really* cool? When it's time to Take Your Daddy to School!"